Café Dog

Tails of West Cornwall

Written and Illustrated by Rosemary Horne

Thank you to David and Philippa, Emma, Becca, Mr Thomas, Nicholas, Scamp, Beaufort, the llamas and rheas. A special thank you to Aggie who inspired this book. All other characters in this publication are fictitious and any resemblance to real persons, past or present, is purely coincidental.

Rosemary Horne was born and brought up in West Penwith. She lives with her husband David and successfully designs and publishes greeting cards and calendars based on her own original artwork. Café Dog is Rosemary's first book and it reflects her love of Cornwall, nature and dogs.

First published 2013 by Penzart
This edition published 2013

A catalogue record for this book is available from the British Library

ISBN 978-0-9927076-0-6

For Mum with love

Contents

Introduction

The magical magnetic pull towards St Just, sweeps the traveller into a time-lost Celtic land; a land of pale green lichen, granite and salt breeze, a land on the edge of the sea, where windswept hawthorns stretch misshapen branches across moorlands of rich, earthy tones and the air is filled with a sense of belonging.

Here in Cape Cornwall Street, located next to Banjo Cottage, another fine cottage with local stonework, a white barn door, grey slate roofing and chimneys that reach into an ever changing Cornish sky.

Inside the cottage, books for browsing or buying, good food, warmth and welcome; always something to look at, always someone to talk to. This cottage is The Cook Book, but besides the food, drink, people and books there is Aggie, beautiful Aggie the café dog. And so our stories begin.

The Cook Book

The whitewashed walls at the back of The Cook Book are stark against a sometimes cloudless West Penwith sky. Earthenware pots sit beside blue bench seats, a bay tree grows in the corner of the yard.

Fuchsia, pansies and roses add colour to the white paintwork.

A shiny green castor oil plant is positioned by the open kitchen door where the sound of cups, saucers and plates being washed adds to the general homely feel.

The narrow blue door of the outside toilet stands against an old stone wall. Ivy hangs down from this wall, its yellow-clustered and powdery heads bright against contrasting dark green leaves.

Creeping upwards and almost meeting the ivy is honeysuckle, a few sweet-smelling flower heads still blooming at any time of the year.

The walk back to the indoor seated area takes one through the storeroom with its cared for comforting smells of washing and fresh laundry, through the black louvre doors, down a step and into the dining area. Here, one large oval table leaves room for four round tables, a bookcase under the window and another tall bookcase against a whitewashed wall.

Each table has a clean, pressed, white tablecloth. Round blue place mats sit well with the white cloths and a striped mug at the centre of each table is filled with wrapped white and brown sugar. A black pebble marks the table number and a small white vase of freshly picked flowers enhances the whole setting. Nothing could be better than having fresh flowers, although nothing could be better than having a dog on the premises; not any dog, but Aggie.

Exhibitions by various artists add colour and interest to the surroundings encouraging customers to view, discuss or buy. Photographs, paintings or tapestries add a wealth of local artistic skills enriching the customers' visits. A pottery display on a large window ledge sits in the curve of the stairs leading upstairs to three rooms of books; books, quiet, warmth, smart cushions in a well lit alcove and two comfy chairs. The peace is palpable. The chairs could be for customers of course, but mostly I think the chairs are for Aggie. They are matching and the slightly frayed ends of the arms could well go back to Aggie's puppy days.

Aggie is the most sensitive, soft, quiet, silky creature anyone could imagine. She is part collie springer cross, showing the usual traits of intelligence and loyalty, and possibly part Saluki adding a unique mix of poise and grace and a sense of the exotic. It's more than likely Aggie who enriches customers' visits.

Star

Voices could be heard floating up from the busy kitchen; 'new book', 'St Just', 'Aggie'. 'It's full of books here' thought Aggie and didn't give it another thought. Later that evening when she was relaxing in her other home where she lived when not working, David and Philippa spoke to their treasured canine friend. 'Beautiful little dog, you're going to be a star'. Aggie cocked her head as she listened then curled up and went to sleep, dreaming of a sky filled with bright white moonlight and sparkling golden stars.

Kelynack Lady

Many visitors come and go and many locals do the same, but for some, visiting The Cook Book and Aggie is an enjoyable routine and the highlight of their day. A lady comes in from nearby Kelynack. She always likes to sit on one of the high wooden stools by the long wooden table where she can see the brass clock on the wall and the barometer underneath.

This ship's clock once had pride of place on David's fishing boat. While she waits for her order she imagines the mighty seas and the rough working conditions of fishermen. She brings her thoughts back to dry land and has a quick glance through the newspaper while she drinks her hot cappuccino which always comes with a small, round melt-in-the-mouth shortbread. She finishes her freshly baked scone with butter and walks up the stairs to view the books. If Aggie is in her chair, the lady will smooth Aggie's soft silky ears and Aggie will doze as if under a spell. As always, feeling better for her visit, the lady from Kelynack makes her way down the stairs and heads for home with joyful thoughts of the friendly dog in the comfy chair.

The Nans

When Aggie has had enough of sleeping, she likes to patrol. She checks on the daily visitors and the many different canine friends they bring with them. Sometimes people come in without dogs and she thinks this is strange. This visitor didn't have a canine friend with him.

Many places start with 'Nan' meaning valley; Nanjizal, Nanquidno, Nancherrow, Nanjulian, Nancledra. Aggie happened to be in the eating area when a very red faced man burst in through the door. He had been attempting to walk to and through all the 'Nan' places but wasn't used to the undulating Cornish countryside with its ups and downs and twists and turns. He also seemed to be working his way through the entire menu. A bottle of spring water helped reduce his face colour. Aggie watched with a look of consternation on her beautiful face as the man ordered his meal. When he had finished, he ordered another meal and then another. 'Surely this man will burst' she thought and disappeared under a table, clothed in the safety of a white tablecloth.

He paid for his many meals saying he had another ten miles to do. He walked in the direction of Nancherrow Hill and past Bank Square Gallery giving only a cursory glance at the many diverse styles exhibited there. He walked past Holly House and was too full to notice Thalia's Cottage set back from the road through the clipped hedge archway and the small crab apple tree just inside the gate. His walk past Nancherrow Studio took him into the curve of the road, past the box on the hedge with anemones and strings of onions set out for sale and into Nancherrow. He would have to do Nanjizal tomorrow after a hearty breakfast. By now, Aggie realised it was safe to emerge from under the table.

Reading

Only a few clever dogs know how to read. Aggie is one of them. From an early age, she would look at the sign on the black louvre doors, she would stare at it, study it. The lettering looked strange. 'Push' said the sign on the doors. Soon, Aggie worked out what to do and very gently pushed the doors with her wet nose. She was now through to the storeroom and the outside area, a place with new smells and things to discover. The sign is not on the door to go back in the other way, and much as Aggie would have loved to practise her reading skills on door signs, with a confident push she always found her way back into the café area.

Mr Thomas' Hat

From her privileged upstairs position, Aggie looked through the cottage windows. It was a windy day and people swayed like stripped willow trying to keep upright.

Because of the strong wind, Mr Thomas was having difficulty with his morning walk to Bank Square. He always wore a hat, but today that hat did not want to stay on Mr Thomas' head. A spirited gust whipped the hat from his head. St Just had never seen Mr Thomas move so fast. Waving his stick in the air, he ran in pursuit of his hat back down Cape Cornwall Street. Aggie watched. The hat kept on rolling, spinning and rolling like a piece of navy blue tumbleweed. Past The Cook Book it rolled, past the Gallery next door, past Cape Cornwall School and all the way to Cape Cornwall. There, it skimmed across the cold Atlantic waters like a prize skimmer. There was no stopping it. Once a Cornish wind takes hold there's no say in the matter.

Poor Mr Thomas was defeated. At ninety three years old he was tired out from his unexpected exertions. He made his way back up Cape Cornwall Street thinking how cold his head was. His good head of hair wasn't enough to keep him warm. Meanwhile, Aggie had performed her louvre door trick, made straight for a box of hats in the storeroom and returned to the window with a hat in her mouth, looking for Mr Thomas. There were several hats to choose from but Aggie selected a dog-tooth check. As he came into sight, hatless and weary, Aggie attracted his attention by placing her paw on the window.

Now when Mr Thomas takes his daily walk and sits a while on the seat in Bank Square, he tells passers-by the story of his hat. He is content to stroll from his home to Bank Square, returning with a pasty in his bag. He is proud to wear Aggie's hat, the dog-tooth check matching his shirt. I'm not sure if he knows, but they do say if you look out to sea at the Brisons, the small peak protruding from the rock is Mr Thomas' hat.

Cream Teas

A local tour guide would often call in and today he had a party of Japanese visitors with, of course, the obligatory cameras. Aggie thought the language sounded very strange. She wasn't sure whether to run, or bask in the attention she was getting from this party. Cameras were tilted this way and that, held at arms' length and Aggie was photographed. Aggie was photographed sitting, Aggie was photographed standing, she was photographed beside the table and underneath the table. The books were photographed and so were the salt and pepper pots. Of course, when the cream teas arrived, the preference was to take pictures rather than eat. How to tackle the cream teas seemed to be a mystery to all of them especially with the addition of a saffron bun on the plate. The tour guide was on hand to show them how to cut the scone, add the jam and then the cream. Aggie patrolled in her version of invisible mode hoping for a crumb. Most people know that Aggie is not to be fed from the tables. Aggie knows this too but she still enjoys practising her look of expectation every now and again.

Jolie and Mum

One day a little girl came into The Cook Book with her Mum. The girl's brother stayed outside eyeing up the vehicles parked along the street. He was only eight but knew all about engine sizes, gear boxes, cambelts and catalytic converters. By now, Jolie and her Mum were seated at the freshly organized table. Choosing was hard for Jolie; so much to choose, so many possibilities. She was only six, so her Mum tried to coax her into making a decision. Her lovely patient Mum started to get a tiny bit impatient. She had had a full morning doing a hundred things and knew she had gone too long without food. Aggie patrolled, wondering whether to watch tables and food or to sit with her books and of course, Jolie noticed her.
After much waiting and wondering, a little girl's voice could just be heard over the other customers. 'I would like ……….a dog' quickly adding 'please'. She knew if she put 'please' on the end of words, things were more likely to materialise.

Meanwhile her brother Tom had decided which car he was going to own, where he was going to work and what colour his boiler suit would be when he became a trained mechanic. Mum and daughter Jolie enjoyed their meal. Tom decided his mouth and stomach needed more attention than cars and joined them. No more is said about dogs .... for now anyway.

After paying and thanking the staff for their tasty meal, Mum and children step out into the fresh salty air of Cape Cornwall Street. 'Dog' whispers Jolie, 'I would like a ……dog'. Old Mrs Medlin who happened to be passing by, overhears the whisper. Her sense of compassion is thin like her frame, and her ears are sharp like her tongue. 'We can't always have what we want when we want it' she rasped. Her lined skin seemed to crinkle as she spoke. 'It's a harsh world' she croaked, and disappeared towards Boswedden Road, her green hat pressed down firmly on her head. No black pointed hat thought Tom, but he still couldn't help standing there open mouthed saying 'Is that a real witch?' Some say Medlin by name, meddling by nature. Some of us don't listen to witch stories. We know things can be different. We know things can be good. Meanwhile indoors, the people looked at the books and the books looked at the people.

Thursday

Everyone in Cape Cornwall Street knows when it's Thursday. The strains of trumpet can be heard struggling over the slate tiled rooftops, the chimneys and into the nearby fields. Dogs start howling but nobody complains. One day, Jack will be there with the best of them in the local band. Before his lesson with Mrs Angove in her small cottage further down the street, Jack calls into The Cook Book. He loves dogs and always makes a fuss of Aggie. Every Thursday his order is always the same. Whatever time of day it is, the All Day Breakfast with Cornish free range eggs (and extra mushrooms) is always available for Jack to order. There's a lot of blowing to be done so he needs sustenance to keep him and the trumpet going. Aggie looks on, wondering when it's time for her tea. Meal finished and ready for anything, Jack walks to his lesson and everyone in Cape Cornwall Street battens down the hatches. Dogs join in with their Grade III canine version of music. Lesson over, Jack walks home clutching his Grade III Associated Board music, his trumpet safe in its case.
Once home, his Mum always cooks him her special All Day Breakfast (with extra mushrooms). 'There Jack, you're a growing lad and you need more than fresh St Just air to play a trumpet'.

Back at The Cook Book, warmth and delicious smells drift into the street. Whenever the white barn door opens, another waft of homeliness stops passers-by in their tracks as they sniff the air, sometimes peering in through the windows to find the source of the aroma. Their owners do the same.

Pot of Tea

Old Mr and Mrs Olds always step in through the door as though they don't have the right to exist. It's the same every Friday. Mrs Olds has her hair done and while she's under the dryer, Mr Olds has his usual quiet ten minutes in the Church. With his shopping bag over his arm, he buys bread from the local baker then sits on the seat in Bank Square, content just to look, surveying the scene he's known for so many years. At The Cook Book, Emma greets them with a smile and after the hubbub of coats, bags and umbrellas, she takes their order. Mr and Mrs Olds study the menu as though they truly intend to order something different. After much deliberation they come to a decision. Emma, of course, already knows what the order will be. 'I think we'll just have a pot of tea please' says Mr Olds in his most polite voice. They liked everything about this place, mostly the wrapped sugar but mainly Aggie. There were no sugar cubes left out in bowls for sticky fingers to play with and no sugar grains in bowls for people to sneeze on. You can't be too careful at their age. Mr Olds paid for their pot of tea and Mrs Olds always left with a chiffon scarf placed lightly over her newly set hair. Aggie always came to see them. They were such kind, gentle people and Aggie knows good people when she sees them.

Dogs

Jolie's lovely Mum thought she would have a look round at some dogs; just out of interest of course. Well, there were big dogs, little dogs, barking dogs, sleeping dogs, yapping dogs, scrapping dogs, howling dogs, yowling dogs, black dogs and yellow dogs, round dogs and found dogs, pack dogs and mellow dogs, white dogs and light dogs, dotty dogs and spotty dogs, tiny dogs and whiny dogs but there were no Aggie dogs. There were dogs waiting and watching, dogs watching and hoping. This didn't mean this wonderful collection of dogs didn't have homes to go to. Goodness no, there's a dog out there for everyone.

Sky Animals

Sometimes when Aggie has had enough of cooking and reading, she likes to stare out of the cottage windows looking for her sky animals. They always appeared on cloudy days, floating along and disappearing out of sight into endless stretches of big blue skies; horses and dragons travelling at speed, a cloud menagerie silent and transient, scudding across the West Country sky. They seemed to make very long journeys as Aggie waited in vain for them to return.

Pipit

Pipit sits quietly beneath the clean white tablecloth covering the round table. Pipit is a black and white collie cross. She had had an early start from Bristol that morning with her owner Jay. Jay likes to indulge his passion for birdwatching. His Mum knew from the moment he was born that he would love birds and chose his name in keeping with the family tradition of choosing names from nature. Jay of course, did the same for his dog. Jay loves this part of the world and tries to do everything he can before returning, and that includes having a Cook Book Breakfast. He had already walked to Cot Valley and visited Nanquidno. At Cot Valley he was delighted to see a great spotted woodpecker undecided about boring into a telegraph pole, and long-tailed tits darting between twigs on a silver-grey blackthorn bush, their high-pitched tsee-tsee-tsee piercing the early morning quiet. At Nanquidno, Pipit stayed close by Jay's side as they heard the throaty kwaark, kwaark, kwaark of glossy black ravens and watched their fast acrobatic flight.

Buzzards circled overhead, their distinctive keeee-keeee first alerting Jay to their presence.

They saw the twist and turn of choughs in playful flight, wing tips sweeping and slicing the air; their call, a strong defiant tone marking their successful return.

Pipit had lapped up a long drink of water from the bowl just inside the white barn door and was happy to be a very well behaved dog as always. Aggie loved meeting people, she loved meeting dogs especially those with stories of faraway places. Aggie stayed with Pipit under the table for a while just listening.

While Jay waited for his breakfast, he placed his Swarovski binoculars to one side of his place setting and studied his Collins Guide to Birds. After breakfast he planned to head for Marazion marshes where he had heard he might get a glimpse of a spotted crake. Marazion seemed to be one of those faraway places to Aggie and she was happy to listen and return to the peace of her books. Anyway, the breakfast had arrived and it was Pipit's turn to emerge from under the table and stare at her master, ever hopeful while he ate.

'Not for dogs Pipit' said Jay as he tucked into two fried eggs, two rashers of smoked bacon, two Cornish sausages, baked beans, mushrooms, grilled tomato, two slices of toast, butter and marmalade and a pot of tea.

Outside, after breakfast, Jay put his rucksack on the floor and reached into the little compartment he kept separately for Pipit. Out came a big, meaty, liver-flavoured chew. 'There you are Pipit' said Jay. 'That should keep you going'. Pipit loved these chews and looked at him, grateful that she hadn't been left out after all. After much chewing and gnawing and another long drink of water, Pipit and Jay make their way to Marazion marshes.

Proper Job

Resting and dozing in her comfy chair, Aggie is suddenly stirred from her relaxed state. She can hear noises and looks up in alarm at the windows. Outside, something is trying to get in, something is attacking her windows. She jumps down from her chair so she can watch from a safer viewpoint. There, a wet bristle-headed monster with a long thin body lunges at the outside panes. Up and down it goes, forwards and backwards, trying to get in, slap, scrape, brush, slide. Unlike Aggie's gentle sky animals, this thing is aggressive and it worries her. It scrubs the windows and all the while, water flows from its head. Aggie knew the windows were shut securely but wasn't convinced this wet bristle-headed monster wouldn't be able to get in.

The monster soon stopped its attack and gradually retreated. With all that effort it must be very tired thought Aggie. Downstairs, all windows cleaned, Becca hands Dan a cup of tea. Dan is a man of few words. 'Proper job' says Dan, 'Proper job'. Aggie yawns and goes back to sleep but with one eye open just in case.

Pass

It was Thursday. The results of Jack's music exam were out. At The Cook Book, before going for his lesson, Jack placed his usual order. Aggie could smell delicious food being cooked. Jack finished his meal and went to the counter to pay and was told 'It's on the house'. Trumpet sounds continued to emanate from Mrs Angove's cottage, but now he was working towards his next exam, all of Cape Cornwall Street held its collective breath for an improvement. After his lesson, Jack made his way home, his trumpet safe in its case, The Associated Board of the Royal Schools of Music Grade IV pieces held firmly and proudly in his other hand. At home, his Mum cooked her special All Day Breakfast (with extra mushrooms), as usual on the house.

Bank Holiday

Another Bank Holiday. The possibility of rain becomes a probability. Rain hits and pits the mixed compost in the flower tubs, forcing clods of earth to land in muddy heaps on the pavements. Rivulets run from Bank Square all the way down to the sea. Aggie looks out from the comfort of her dry home. She sees umbrellas, lots of umbrellas, all sizes and colours. The umbrellas are under her window and people are under the umbrellas and they're sitting at the blue bench seats outside the white barn door. David holds an umbrella for Emma as she ventures into the outdoor seating area with cream teas, serving stoic figures shrouded in wholly ineffective plastic capes.

'We often do this al dente don't we Jean' said one of the party. 'Alfresco Mother', 'Where dear?', 'Outside Mother', 'That's what I said dear.'

And the rain fell down spitting off the top of the scones like scattered grit, Cornish rain topping up their cups of tea and sliding down their backs. David and Emma are glad to go back in. It wasn't necessarily the gutter's fault, it was just overloaded; it couldn't take any more. There's only so much water a gutter can hold before overspilling and overspill it did. The umbrellas couldn't take the weight of the water from the overloaded gutter and the stoic party couldn't take the weight of the water from the overloaded umbrellas. Soaked is an understatement.

Aggie could hear the commotion. She could see the commotion. She was glad she wasn't part of the commotion. She was thankful her walk had been delayed so she could keep her coat and paws dry. The customers, a little crestfallen, return to the dry, clutching what they can salvage of their cream teas. Towels are found from somewhere, teas are replenished and Aggie makes an entrance making everything right.

Mrs Tregear

Piran sat with Granny Bray. He's just finished his delicious strawberry milkshake, ice cold and frothy but not too cold that it hurt his teeth and not too frothy that he couldn't suck up any liquid through the bendy straw.

He couldn't help making the gurgling noises when he got to the bottom of the glass and because Granny Bray was taking so long with her cups of tea, he couldn't help swinging his legs past the chair and playing with the salt and pepper pots. Mrs Tregear breezed by. 'It's very important not to upset the equilibrium young man' she said and patted his head a little too heavily. Piran left Granny Bray with her fourth cup of tea and followed Aggie through the louvre doors hoping to find the equilibrium in the outside toilet. At least he would be able to say sorry although he wasn't sure what he was sorry for.

Another customer who was ready to pay for her meal noticed her purse was missing. Taking charge, Mrs Tregear says loudly 'We need to do some sequential backtracking my dear' patting her on the head, even though she was grown up, and organized everyone to backtrack sequentially. Aggie had noticed this customer browsing through the books earlier and remembered seeing a small red purse by one of the chairs upstairs. Aggie goes upstairs, carefully picks up the purse in her mouth and steps down the stairs so quietly that nobody notices her. The purse is found but everyone is too busy backtracking with Mrs Tregear at the helm. Eventually someone notices Aggie waiting patiently with the found purse. The 'good dog' 'clever dog' compliments are manifold and Aggie bathes in the praise bestowed upon her.

The Big Jelly

Emma and Becca were discussing jelly making and the merits of cubes or crystals, mixed flavours or plain flavours, sharp, sweet or tangy flavours, beetroot or cochineal colouring, gelatin or carrageenan thickening. The big jelly would need a big mould then the work could begin. Windows open, sleeves rolled up, the big jelly was under construction and heading for the big set. Piran was in with Granny Bray. As usual he had finished his milkshake and looked in dismay at the full teapot knowing how long he might have to sit there. Piran was a good little boy. He loved his gran but he would much rather be exploring at Porth Nanven finding dinosaur eggs and shapes and faces in the shiny wet yellow ochre rocks, especially as he had noticed Mrs Tregear was in again today.

At the table next to him a grown up customer was nearing the end of her milkshake. She looked at Piran and smiled. To his delight, she wiped the bendy straw round the inside of the glass so as not to miss any of the froth and gurgled loudly as the last drops of milk disappeared. 'Have a little decorum child' said Mrs Tregear, thinking it must have been Piran. 'But I'm full up' he said and ducked under the table pretending to pick up a napkin so as to avoid any head patting. Unfortunately as he ducked, the big jelly was making its way past the tables on a large silver platter held high above Becca's head. Aggie followed not wanting to miss out on anything. Well, if the lady hadn't gurgled her milkshake and Mrs Tregear hadn't said what she did, and if Piran hadn't ducked under the table, who knows? But she did, and she did and he did and the big jelly toppled. And of course, it toppled from a great height. Poor Aggie.

Following behind the big jelly, Aggie became the big jelly. A soft jelly heap landed on poor Aggie's head and slid to the tip of her beautiful nose.
Wet dogs and messy dogs always become shaking dogs. Aggie was ready for the big shake. Her head and body seemed to work in opposite directions; a special thing dogs do called rotational oscillation, in turn creating jelly spin-offs. Dog lovers knew this would happen and dived under tablecloths just in time. Those not knowing anything about dogs remained seated then wished they did know something about dogs. Lime green jelly was everywhere!
Aggie was led through to the back. Nobody was cross with her; it wasn't her fault the big jelly fell out of the sky. Piran looked to others to gauge the tone of the situation. Customers emerged from under the tables. Granny Bray wiped jelly off her face, the milkshake lady winked at Piran and all anyone could do was laugh. Aggie soon came back through the louvre doors and was paid so much attention she had to go upstairs to the peace of her books. Some of the jelly spin-offs went quite a distance. It is said there have been sightings on the leeward side of Pendeen lighthouse, green blobs stuck fast like little fluorescent jewels.

Lost

Aggie had canine friends all over St Just. There was a bit of a mizzle when her cousins took off from South Bosvargus Farm. The puppies had recently been to the vet so were ready to roam the big wide world. This world was a bit too big and too wide for one of them. On the walk, a fog closed in. This was a thick fog, a damp white-out. There was no going left or right. There was total disorientation. People bumped into each other and nobody knew which direction they were going in. Mr Tregurtha who lived at Tregeseal ended up in Zennor. However clever, whatever senses we think we might have, a thick fog filling the air like wet pastry will always put us right off track. It was no wonder that one of the canine party disappeared. One minute there, the next lost, a helpless little puppy lost in the worsening fog. Grass was wet underfoot, granite rocks appeared from nowhere and birds stopped singing.

Aggie couldn't rest. She knew something was wrong. Up and down the stairs she went, in and out through the louvre doors, up to her chairs and back down again. She knew before word went round that one of the Bosvargus puppies was missing. At her first chance, Aggie slipped out through the white barn door and made off. Although the fog was still treacherous, Aggie was able to negotiate her way. She knew instinctively where she had to go. She took herself down Cape Cornwall Street, turned left and followed the sign to Cot Valley. This was her patch, but this time she wasn't interested in beaches or boulders. She continued down the narrow road towards Porth Nanven beach. Back at The Cook Book concern was great. Worried staff and customers waited for Aggie to return. The worry was so great that customers didn't want to eat and the cook didn't want to cook. Nobody could concentrate. The Cook Book had come to a standstill.

Found

In the field behind Porth Nanven Barn, guarded by mum, dad and baby llama was the frightened, bedraggled, lost, tired, hungry puppy. These beautiful creatures, the llamas, had sensed something was wrong and kept the puppy safe and warm with their soft breath and their luxurious wool.

The rheas in the field on the other side of the road stopped pecking at their food buckets and ran to their gate to see what was going on. Aggie knew she would find the lost puppy here. How did she know? She just did. These were her well loved familiar places close to her home. She left the llamas to nibble the wet grass on the hedge and carefully guided the puppy back to the safe and cosy Cook Book.

Word went round that the puppy was safe. All puppies are special, but this one had survived the fog, the wet and the cold and she was very hungry. The arrival of two wet but safe dogs was cause for celebration. Customers ate and the cook cooked. After some soft chicken pieces mixed with rice and a bowl of warm milky tea all made specially by a very relieved Philippa, the puppy had the strength to follow Aggie up the stairs.

Surrounded by books, Aggie and the puppy rest and sleep in warmth and safety, and in the peace of the upstairs rooms, dream a little of good things ahead. All these books make Aggie a very knowledgeable dog. Perhaps the little puppy will be a clever dog too. The puppy slept soundly but Aggie could hear voices from downstairs and they sounded apologetic. 'I've got a gerbil', 'My cat wouldn't like it', 'My boyfriend's allergic'. Nobody saw Jolie and her Mum standing at the counter. 'I haven't got a gerbil a cat or a boyfriend, I'm only six and nobody's 'lergic' said Jolie with a look of wonder and hope on her upturned face. Well, it did the trick. At a later date and after discussions with South Bosvargus Farm, arrangements were made for Jolie to be the proud owner of the little puppy.

Leswidden Pool

Chunks and pieces of white quartz lie scattered at the water's edge. The pool is as blue as the blue of the china clay working days, now only possible when the weather, the sky and the clouds are just right. Only then does the pool take on the unique china clay blue. Herring gulls float and dive in this very deep pool making it their own, bobbing on the water's surface like hundreds of white sculpted origami models.

Tom had discovered his friend's Dad owned cars, lots of cars. He will never forget the day at the old clay works. The cars were kept in a very large shed. Together, they unlocked the padlock on the old wooden doors and Zac's Dad pulled back the doors to reveal a gleaming red classic Cadillac. The sight, the feel and the smell of this discovery would stay with Tom for ever. The chrome was without tarnish and the cream leather seats were beeswaxed to a soft supple finish, making the long front bench seat without divisions appear to go on for ever.

Two friendly dogs from Higher Bostraze Farm ran up to Tom hoping to join in. They were used to farm vehicles but this was something different. They'd always had front row driving positions on tractors and pickups so why not on a shiny, spotless Cadillac. Tom was allowed to sit in the front seat and study the controls but with so much to take in and with shorter arms than a grown up, the door was left open. And there they were, right beside him, the two Bostraze dogs sitting bolt upright, staring ahead and ready to go.

The inquisitive jackdaws on the nearby single stack jumped and danced, playing their games of hide-and-seek in the cracks and grooves of the irregular stones, their sharp chat-chat-chat echoing around the sunken pool.

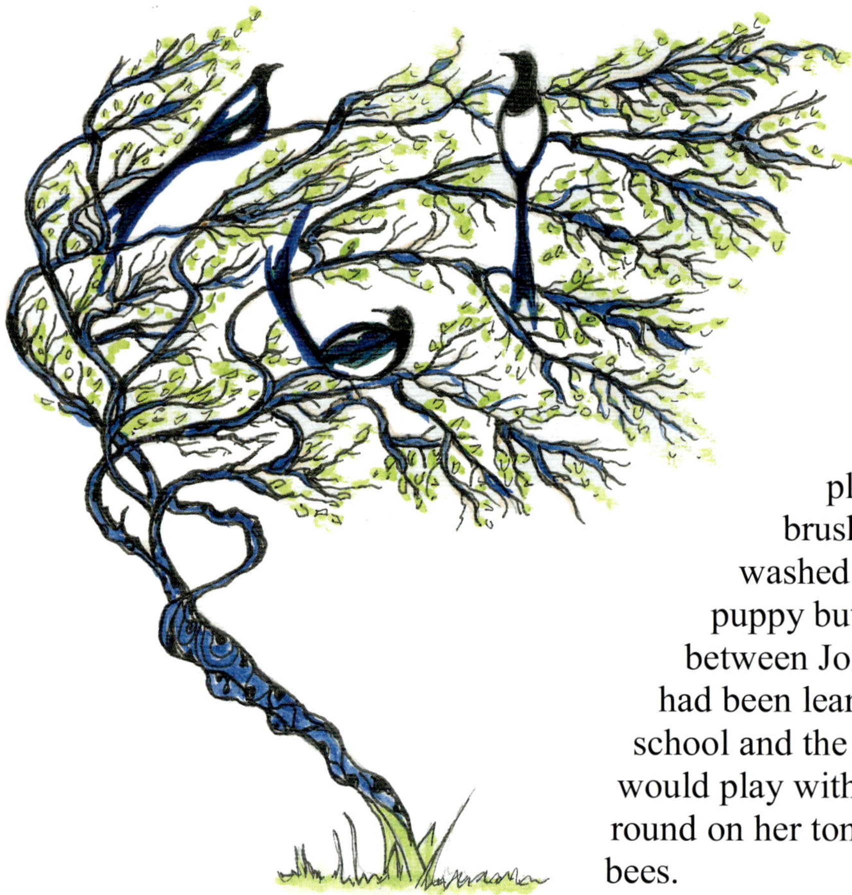

Name

Jolie's Mum was busy trying to get through her '100 things to do today' list. Tom was occupied with his quest for car knowledge and that probably included riding around in Cadillacs. Jolie played with her puppy and brushed her coat to a newly washed shine. Everyone loved the puppy but there was a special bond between Jolie and her little dog. Jolie had been learning about the letter 'z' in school and the sound it made and she would play with the zzzzz's rolling them round on her tongue like so many angry bees.

She knew what she was going to call the puppy but she wanted to make her announcement at The Cook Book. She wanted Aggie to be there.

Jolie's Mum always counted magpies, often when they were crouching into the wind on stunted hawthorns, their iridescent tails flashing purple and green. One for sorrow, two for joy, three for a girl ….. 'A baby girl puppy' thought Mum and continued with her jobs.

When Jolie and her Mum next visited The Cook Book with the puppy, Aggie didn't have to see who was walking in through the white barn door, she just knew. People remarked that the little dog looked just like Aggie when she was a puppy, such a fine head and a beautiful glossy coat and a tail that wagged all the cutlery off the well laundered tablecloths. For the announcement, Jolie held her puppy close and made sure that Aggie was close by and everyone had stopped eating and drinking.

With a confidence only a six year old with a new dog can have, Jolie announced 'My dog is to be called Maggie Mizzle'.

Everyone clapped and resumed eating and drinking. Jolie knew her puppy had been lost and found in the fog and she knew mizzle wasn't quite the same as fog. But saying Maggie fog dog didn't sound as grown up as Maggie Mizzle.

All Is Well

Generally in Bank Square things look good. The town clock chimes when it is supposed to and the smell of freshly cut grass at the Plen-an-Gwarry filters into the fresh, salty air. Beaufort the magnificent Leonberger guards his property from behind the gate, his deep barks resonating around the square. Scamp the Parson Russell terrier sits patiently by his water bowl, waiting for Nicholas to finish one of his fine detailed paintings. Flower tubs overflow with plants, a profusion of colour and blooms; orange begonias, bright blue lobelia, petunias, geraniums and marigolds.

A soothing, salty breeze blows in from the deep ruffled waters of the Atlantic, a healing balm permeating the core of St Just and nearby villages.

Mr Thomas' hat is a little more weather-beaten due to its location but is still visible on the Brisons.

Nowadays people stand and listen to the much improved tuneful trumpet sounds floating from the direction of Mrs Angove's cottage.

Ride

In the distance, a gleaming red Cadillac can be seen negotiating the narrow lanes. Tom, still only little at eight, sits on the passenger seat and is just visible through the wide windscreen. Beside him, two Bostraze dogs sit bolt upright, staring ahead enjoying the ride. The soft summer sounds of California Dreamin' fade further away at every bend in the winding road, the car's occupants leaning into each other at every turn of the wheel. The rear fins of the vehicle almost nudge the hedges where curious cows look in surprise over lichen encrusted stones.

Happy Birthday

October, the month of Aggie's birthday, brings with it some clear sunny days, days when strength and colour seep back into fading blooms, when sounds become softer and people smile. Aggie loves her birthday walk. With her lead attached to her little leather collar, she walks with David, taking in all the sights and smells.

Washing hangs from lines on poles in back gardens. Cottages nestle on a nearby hill. The sky is filled with birds. Cows drink from troughs and graze in the sunlit fields. The quiet falls on the ears, even a whisper would break the spell. Only the sounds of starlings' wings can be heard as they whirr by on their squat-tailed flight and all the while, the stream runs gently down to the sea.

Starlings on the network of telegraph wires whistle and gurgle their guttural songs.

Orange marigolds grow next to cabbages and October roses thrive on their almost leafless stalks.

In Bosorne Road, a fig tree grows in a pot in a back yard, jackdaws chat-chat-chat and the bright but sparse flower heads of montbretia display their colours to the world before the seed heads form. A few blackberries remain on their thorny branches.

Aggie pauses at an old wooden gate and looks at the view stretching over fields to the sea. Rooks forage in the newly harvested fields and in the distance there is a low-pitched hum of a light aircraft taking off from Land's End Aerodrome. It is but a small jolt into the world of people travelling, people changing places, people changing lives. Bleached white umbellifers stand tall, their full black-seeded heads ready to burst from their temporary casing. Thin twines of bindweed curl upwards, still attached to the now hollow stems of hedge parsley. Aggie passes the fields with the llamas and rheas. The llamas are busy with grass nibbling, long lashes framing their deep brown caring eyes. The rheas peck at their food buckets. They all communicate in their own way. All the while the stream runs gently down to the sea and the starlings whistle. Young ferns grow from stone walls. Ornamental artichokes grow tall against the blue October sky. The few heads on the bleached stems of cornflowers are still a piercing blue against the fiery orange of nasturtiums.

Beehives shine white in the warm October sun and in the field behind, buttercups form bright patches in the green grass.

Pansies adorn the top of a wall, the mauve of some, complementing the vivid deep purple of others, a deep purple richer than any regal or papal robe. Pink valerian although not profuse, still adds to the character of the grey stone wall. A fig tree grows from the hedge and trumpet lichen grows from old grey Cornish stones.

The huge leathery gunnera leaves encroach into the narrow road. Old withered leaves lie on the ground like prehistoric skin. Aggie knows she is close to the beach.
The tide is out. Like a gazelle she races alongside the incoming tide, her lithe, slim body almost flying with boundless energy. She watches a cormorant diving into the waves and she looks for the seal who likes to play games; shiny, black, watching, then gone, only to pop up further along the coast. The seal looks for Aggie and plays the game.

Aggie runs over long, glistening seaweed, thick slippery strands waving like Medusa's head at the water's edge. She sees small birds dipping and darting amongst the rocks and a grey wagtail, its yellow rump bright against pebbles and dry white stones tide washed and sparkling in the afternoon light. As the clear, cold tide ebbs and flows, wet stones shine and pools form in the soft-grained patterned sand.

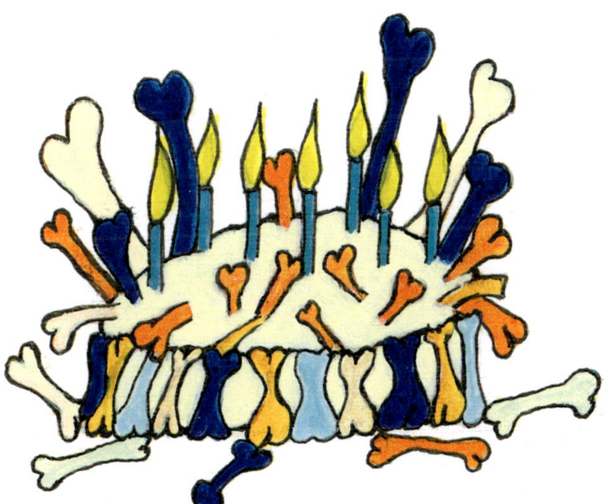

It was a surprise of course but a special canine birthday cake waited for Aggie when she returned. While David and Aggie had the special birthday walk, Philippa had been busy making a cake adding all Aggie's favourite tastes. It was like a canine version of Starry Gazey pie. Instead of fish heads and tails poking out of the top of the pie, Aggie could see bones and chews.

Happy Birthday Aggie!

Happy Dog

Aggie's birthday walk was the best walk in the world but the day is not yet over. At home, Aggie hears the cereal box being taken from the cupboard and the clink of her bowl against the kitchen worktop. David prepares her late supper, one Weetabix with cold milk and no sugar for Aggie to enjoy before going to bed. Philippa places the bowl where Aggie can reach it. It's the same every night. Aggie snuffles in her bowl and where the milk hasn't soaked into the dry crispy Weetabix cake, she sneezes occasionally as the soft, dry bits tickle her nose. Every night she licks her bowl clean. She loves this night-time routine and is only happy to go to bed after her Weetabix.

Aggie is as content and happy as any dog could be. Safe and warm in her cosy bed, she closes her sleepy eyes and dreams of a sky filled with bright white moonlight and sparkling golden stars.

Sleep well beautiful dog, another day tomorrow.